THE STORY
BERKLEY THE GURU
SAVES THE DAY! ©

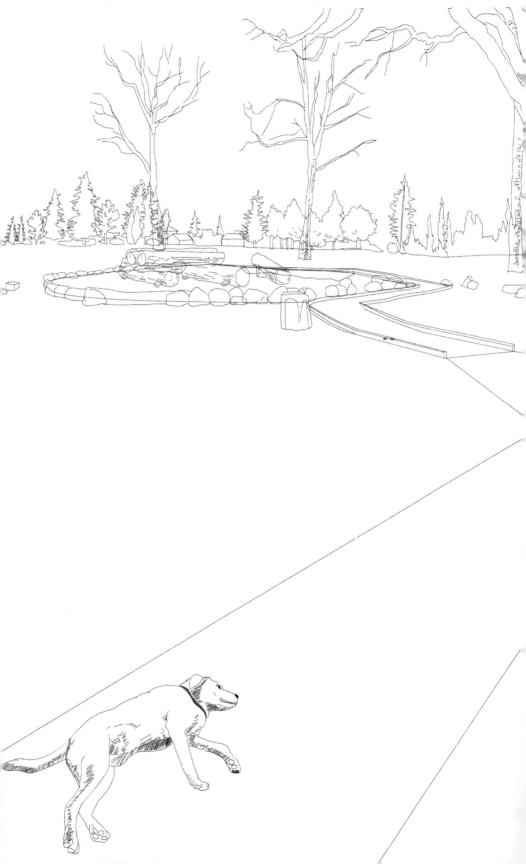

ISBN # 978-0-578-49227-8

Printed in United States of America

First Printing, 2019

Chapter 1:
Who is
BERKLEY ?

Hello, I am Berkley the Guru. I am a "career change" guide dog for the blind. Career change means that the people at the Guide Dogs for the Blind decide which of their young dogs they raise have the right stuff to become a guide dog. Being a guide dog is a big responsibility and is a demanding career for a dog, so the good people at the Guide Dogs for the Blind make sure which dogs would enjoy this type of life and which would not (which is me!).

First, let me tell you a little about myself. I am a 6-year old yellow Labrador boy who was born at the Guide Dogs for the Blind. After 9 months, it was decided by the good people at the Guide Dogs for the Blind, that I should be a "career change" dog. This means, instead of going to work as a guide dog, I would instead be put up for adoption and hopefully soon be placed with a loving family enjoying life as a family dog. Soon after, I was lucky enough to get adopted at 10 months old by a great family.

    One of the main reasons I think I was not an ideal candidate for the demands of a guide dog life is because I love to flop (yes, flop), or as my dad calls it, the "Big Flop." The act of flopping can be described as a sudden or slow build up of emotion when I decide I don't want to do something and enough is enough, so I flop wherever I am. I could be on a walk in the park, on the grass, on the neighborhood street, at the local hardware store, at my dad's favorite cappuccino café, it doesn't matter. I flop anywhere!

Most of the time, if you know me well enough, (like my dad and mom) you can see my "big flop" coming and avoid it before I actually flop. It's usually a good idea to try to avoid my flop. Once I flop, I am pretty darn hard to get back up and I am certainly not going to get back up without some special treats. At that point, it becomes a fun game between me and my dad and what I can get away with and how many treats I am going to get!

Usually, you can prepare for my flop if you are paying attention, since I usually give you a little look. That look, while on my walk, basically means, 'Hey, Dad. I don't want to go that way,' or 'I am ready for home.' Even better, my little warning look which means I am about to flop could also be because I see a furry friend approaching that I want to meet. Usually it goes a little like this, 'Dad, I'm about to flop. Don't try to lead me a different way. Here I go! Try to stop me!" ...and FLOP!

Most of the time I like to flop because I've had my fun and now I'm done and want to chill out and wait for some of my dog friends to walk by. Other times, I am just playing games with my dad for treats and drive him a little crazy (heehee). But the most important thing is because, I am Berkley, and I do and go where I want to go and that's why I take control and FLOP!!!!!! I am Berkley, and I am showing my independence, and if I don't want to do something, you can't make me!!! I guess that's another reason why it was decided that I might not be a great guide dog for the blind. (teehee).

Chapter 2:
My New
Family

When I arrived at my new home it took a little while to settle in with my new family and new brother (a border collie/blue heeler mix named BooBoo, who, by the way, was a senior). I really started to enjoy my new life with my family. Walking, playing, snuggling and eating!

At first, I was still a little sad that I couldn't be a guide dog because I didn't want to be a failure. But soon I realized that not becoming a guide dog is never about failing but finding the right fit for the doggy and the human. Turns out, it was a great decision for me too, and I settled into a great life, but as an ordinary family member, not a specialized, trained guide dog.

But as I grew up, I started to ask myself, 'If I wasn't cut out to be a Guide Dog, what was I cut out for? Did I have any special talents?' I started to really want to find out what my true calling was. I never was sad, but I kept wanting to know if I should be doing something more meaningful with my life. I loved my family and had a great life, but something was missing and I wanted to discover what that was.

I started trying to find if I had any special talents and purpose in life, and even though I loved my family and my life, I always felt that I was destined for something more. But finding your special talent or purpose in life is hard, so I went on with my fun and loving life and hoped it would just come to me eventually.

My brother BooBoo was 10 years my senior. BooBoo, like most herding dogs, loved to be the boss and BooBoo really kept me in line. I guess BooBoo came from a breed that like protecting sheep, and they also loved quiet, order and peace, over everything. So BooBoo went to work every day bossing me around and not letting me get away with anything! I usually just followed his lead and kept calm, but he did occasionally play tug with me and I really enjoyed that. My dad and mom would always step in to let me play so I did get a lot of fun and exercise, but my big brother BooBoo ran a tight ship!

I have been told that since I come from a guide dog heritage that I am naturally more calm and possibly have some therapeutic qualities (whatever that means). I am pretty chill and I guess very calming around other dogs. I get along with everyone and love meeting new dogs. I never bark or cause a scene, I just welcome in a very calm way all my animal friends. I love animals and feel a real kinship with all of them.

   When I meet new dogs or people, they know pretty quickly that I am safe, loving, and approachable. My dad said I have really helped in our neighborhood with other dogs' first socializations. Dogs meeting other dogs for the first time can be stressful, but I have helped since I give off a comforting and soothing energy. My trick is, I make my eyes really soft, then I wag my tail a bit, don't do any sudden moves, and let the new dog or human come to me. Then, we do some gentle sniffing or petting, and sometimes I even flop and let them know I am just chill!

So I started to think, 'Maybe I do have at least one special talent!' My dad says I always put dogs and humans and every other animal at ease. One of my favorite things to do is to flop down as kids flock over to me and gently pet me, give me snuggles, and make a big deal about how cute and soft I am. By the way, I especially like it when they gently stroke my ears.

OLD
EADOWAYE
FARM

I love seeing the chickens, pigs, and cows at the nearby farm we walk by. We are so lucky that in our suburban neighborhood there is a beautiful park with grass, and an old farm with animals on the other side with a walking path between the two. How lucky is that? This farm, at one time, many years ago, I guess, owned all the land where our houses are now. Now all that is left is a quaint farm home, a barn, and a big pasture with a few farm animals enjoying life.

On my many walks, I got to know the animals and would often speak with them. My dad and I are super close. We learned to communicate with each other and I eventually began to understand almost every word he said, and he understood just what my looks I give him mean.

Chapter 3:
Say it
isn't so

One day, I heard one of my animal friends loudly ask for help. I quickly led my dad to the adjacent fence to find out what was going on. I barked softly to communicate with my sheep friends. My friend, Teddy the sheep, answered and told me that a new farmer took over and he wanted to get rid of all the animals. I said, "Oh, no! Why would anyone want to get rid of you?" Teddy said that Maggie, the lead momma piggy, said the new farmer was trying to make a deal to sell all the animals to the local restaurant called Booya Burger Castle.

"What!!!!" I exclaimed, "Why would he do that, and I thought burgers were made with veggies?" Teddy told me, "No, Berkley, most meat and burgers are made, unfortunately, from us animals." I couldn't believe it! My dad never told me that and he always eats burgers, but his are the veggie kind and are super yummy.

I couldn't understand why any humans (who are usually super sweet and I love them) would want to turn my animal friends into food. The humans love me and I love my animal friends, so why do humans harm animals and love me? How can this be? Humans and the animals are my friends. Teddy told me the sad truth that most of the cows, pigs, and chickens are farmed to become hamburgers and hot dogs and wings.

OLD MEADOWAYE FARM

I was so sad I didn't say a word until we got home. Then I asked my dad about it and Dad reluctantly said, "Yes, Berkley, it is true." My dad said, "Berkley you have to understand that many people had to eat meat and animals to survive a long time ago, and unfortunately, the tradition still remains for many today.

"But Berkley, there is also good news that many humans are starting to just eat vegetarian or vegan so animals are not harmed, and more and more people are changing their views and trying to help all animals."

I was confused and asked Dad, "What is a vegan and what is a vegetarian?" He explained that vegetarians eat a vegetable diet with no animal meat, but do eat dairy (cheese, milk, and yogurt). Vegans also eat a vegetable diet with no meat, but follow a stricter 100% plant-based diet with no dairy products.

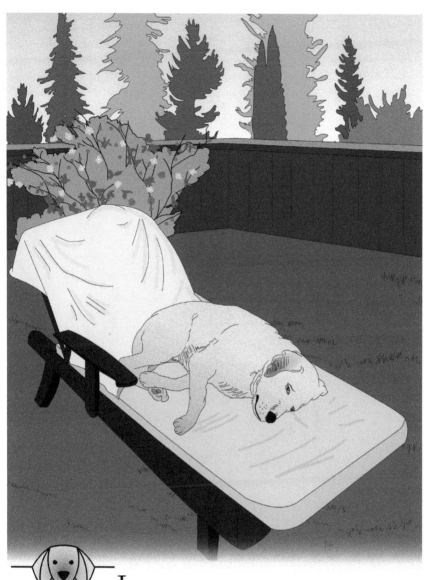

Chapter 4: What to do?

I was so confused and upset, I decided to go to my favorite spot to relax my mind and think. I went outside to the backyard deck to sit on my lounge chair in the sunshine and try to understand all this new scary information. I soon fell into a deep meditative state as I watched through our fence and saw a glimpse of my animal friends in the distance eating hay, playing, and just enjoying their lives.

After about an hour of reflection, in a sudden rush, I had a fantastic warm feeling come over me and that's when it hit me! "That's it, Dad!" I sprang from my chair and ran to get my dad and I was so excited I was doing circles and jumps. "Dad, I know now!" "You know what, Berkley?" my dad asked. "I know what I am here for!" "Berkley," my dad said, "What are you here for?"

"I know this now, **I am Berkley the Guru,** and I am here to speak for and protect my animal friends!"

My dad was very excited, but not surprised. After my meditation, I finally figured out what my purpose was and that I must act. After talking with Dad, he said he would help with anything I needed to save the animals.

Chapter 5:
The Plan

I guess my dad always knew my special love for my animal friends and he said, "Berkley, the first thing we need to do is organize and ask all your human friends in the neighborhood to see if they would be willing to help protect the animals." "Dad, that is great!" I said. "And we can tell them that the animals deserve to live their lives in peace on the farm they grew up on and not sold to some burger restaurant!"

So, Dad and I went door to door, and we also posted the situation on my Twitter and Instagram accounts and asked for volunteers to join the protest.

My dad and I visited as many neighbors as we could. We talked to the people who already knew us and they all said they actually loved me and they wanted to do anything possible to help me and my animal friends.

So, we decided to all meet at the park at 9am and to protest with signs and a mini march up and down the path along the fence of the farm. "Protect the animals, let them be," my human friends proclaimed. "They are not to be sold, they are to be protected!" My fellow dog friends barked in protest and wore signs on their jackets saying, "Free our friends. Animals are not for eating but for loving."

VEGAN BURGER

100 % PLANT BASED

Dad also told me that he thought there was a chance that with the support of the neighbors he could introduce his vegan burgers and vegan hot dogs to Booya Burger Castle, maybe even eventually convincing them to switch to all plant-based burgers so even more animals could be saved. I said, "Dad, I love this plan!"

 contains text in the image:

OLD MEADOWAYE FARM

Animals are our Friends

Save the Animals

Vegan for Animals

Animals are our Friends

Save the Animals

Our protest lasted all day with different human and animal friends of mine coming and going to the park to show their support. The farmer, in the middle of the day, finally came to the fence during the protest and told the crowd that he has every right to sell the animals.

He then told all of us that he has lots of bills to pay and if he didn't make the deal and sell the animals to Booya Burger Castle by tomorrow at 10am he would lose out on the money he needed. The farmer walked back to his home and we were all left sad and feeling helpless. I began racking my brain trying to think of how to save my animal friends before 10am tomorrow came.

By this time, it was very late and my supportive human and animal friends had to go back to their homes for the night. My dad told me that even if the situation looks bleak, to never give up and maybe something good will happen. He told me to always think positive and remember the important thing is the love in you and you are fighting for your friends.

"Berkley, you have also organized a movement to help your friends," my dad said. "No matter what the outcome is, Berkley, you are a hero in many ways."

I liked my dad trying to make me feel good, but honestly I didn't feel very heroic. I actually felt sick to my tummy that my friends were going to get taken and our efforts were not going to be able to stop it.

Dad also told me that he would sit out here with me in the park all night to show support, but I knew he had to pick up my mom at the airport. I said, "I know you would do it, you have done so much and I love you. But Dad, let's go home and I need some rest. There is nothing more we can do tonight."

So, we got home and after my Dad, BooBoo, and I ate a late dinner, my dad was set to leave for the airport around 1130pm to pick up my mom who was flying back from a business trip. BooBoo and I would usually go on the airport run, but I let my dad know I wanted to stay close to home and show my animal friends that I am with them.

Chapter 7:
Act Quickly

After Dad got a couple hours of quick shut-eye, he got up and left to get mommy. I was really restless and unhappy and felt helpless that I couldn't help my friends. I managed to finally drift off to sleep around 3 am but slept downstairs so I could be closer to my animal friends instead of my usual big bed with my mom, Dad and brother upstairs.

All of a sudden, I was awakened around 4 or
5 am, after hearing a loud bang from the farm. I immediately
stared out the window to see if I could figure out what was
happening. I could see a big truck backed up to the farm and
a lot of commotion going on. I also heard a lot of my animal
friends making noises but I couldn't make out what they were
saying. BooBoo came downstairs after hearing my whimpers
and said, "Berkley, you are not going anywhere. You stay here
and your big brother will go check it out."

BooBoo was so smart and resourceful, he knew how to open the back window a certain way with his nose and paw. It was remarkable to see him in action.

I watched my brother run to the corner of our back yard, then make two quick, but amazing jumps, from the raised planting bed to a big stone that he used to spring over the fence. I watched intently, as I could barely see BooBoo move under the cover of the early morning night carefully approaching the farmer's fence.

More commotion was happening with the animals and the big truck. I realized they must be trying to load up and take the animals earlier than 10am like the farmer said, probably to avoid all of us from protesting.

Then, all of sudden, I couldn't see BooBoo but only heard his barks. I couldn't make out what he was saying, only that I could tell he was in trouble. I knew I had to spring into action, but I was scared and had never done anything by myself like this. I wasn't brave or talented like my brother BooBoo. But I knew I had to face my fears and be confident in order to help.

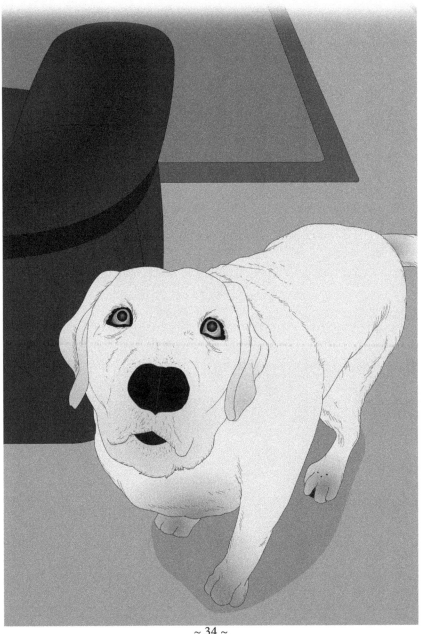

I carefully tried to remember how BooBoo got out, but couldn't waste the time. I ran to the window and nudged it up with my head as hard as possible and it raised just enough for me to run through the screen and quickly over the fence.

W hat I witnessed was so scary. Two big men were forcing my cow, pig, and chicken friends toward the big truck to load them up and take them away.

Chapter 8:
The Big
FLOP

To save the animals, I had to think quickly. I managed to see BooBoo. They had caught him and tethered him with a rope to a post on the other side of the barn. I couldn't decide if I should try to help BooBoo or my other animal friends. At the last second, I had an idea!

I decided to use the only skill I knew I had and did the biggest FLOP I could! I stretched myself out so that nobody could get into the truck. I knew this was only a temporary plan, but I had to do something. Then I saw the two men move towards me. They grabbed me and tried to move me, but I held my ground, stretched out as far as I could along the ground and made myself as heavy as possible, bracing myself for another attempt to move me.

They grabbed me again. This time, they started dragging me as I tried holding my ground. I heard BooBoo protesting in the background, worrying about me. The two men eventually were able to drag me way off to the side. But as they were doing this, I heard my brother spring into action. I saw out of the corner of my eye, BooBoo charging towards all of us. BooBoo was doing what he knew best and what he loved best. He started herding all the animals back into the fenced pasture while the two men were distracted with my flopping.

BooBoo ran like the wind, in circles, gently nipping at some of the animal's feet, corralling them into the pasture one by one. Turns out, while BooBoo was tied up, he could still see everything and knew he needed to help, so he had chewed through his tethered rope. BooBoo, because of his instincts and intelligence, was able to lead the animals by herding them back through the pasture to safety.

Then, before the men could react, BooBoo managed to get all the animals safely back into the pasture, and with all his body weight, shut the big gate until it was finally closed shut.

Then, all of sudden, I saw lights from many flashlights and a lot of commotion as dawn broke. Evidently, my neighborhood human and animal friends had also come to our rescue!

   Probably 20 or 30 of my human neighbors and furry friends were there yelling at the men and seeing if I was okay.

   Then the crowd parted and I saw my dad emerge from the crowd toward me and gave me a big hug and asked if I was okay. I told Dad I was fine and that BooBoo and I managed to stop the farmer, but only temporarily.

Then I got a sudden and powerful urge. I got myself together and walked over to the men and then sat in front of them and stared into their eyes. I used the deepest and most compassionate stare I could at the men. In a matter of seconds, the men's attitude changed as they looked into my eyes.

Then they let out a big sigh and their demeanor changed from being mean to being kind. They, evidently all "woke," (meaning they saw the light of goodness within themselves) and realized they were wrong.

The men instantly realized the care, effort, and love that I and so many had shown to save my animal friends; it changed them. The farmer spoke and said, "I am so sorry. I don't know why I would try to hurt the animals. They should have the same rights as all of us and it is wrong to use them for food."

The farmer went on to explain that, our actions, coupled with my powerful but compassionate gaze, had changed him and his family at the farm. He announced that he and his family would devote themselves in some way to protect all animals.

Chapter 9:
Becoming a
GURU
to help animals

After talking some more with my dad, the farmer and his family agreed to sample my dad's vegan burgers, and after the tasting, loved them! Now, after the farmer's awakening and tasting how delicious vegan burgers can be, the entire family realized there is a better way!

Within a few weeks, the farmer re-opened his farm, but this time as an animal sanctuary/vegan farm. An animal sanctuary is a place where animals are rescued and are safe, protected, and loved just like I am.

The farmer and his family also started to learn about organic farming and the power of plant-based food. They worked hard together while caring for the animals and they planted organic chickpeas, organic tofu, and many other wonderful organic beans and vegetables. The college the farmer's son and his sister decided to go to was a specialized organic vegan cooking school, so after graduating, they began to make the world's best organic vegan patties powered by all the organic vegetables they grew.

The restaurant owner of Booya Burger Castle was even invited to try the patties. He loved them and immediately agreed to start buying them from the farmer's family. He announced he would begin serving an all-vegan menu. It turned out to be a big hit at all his restaurants.

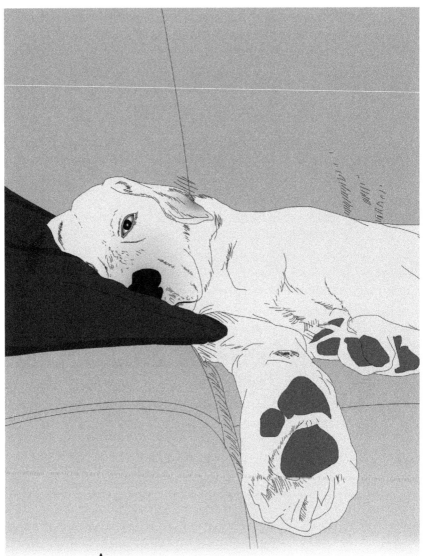

A few weeks later, I sat back at my favorite spot in my backyard as the sun shone through the sky and warmed my fur while looking at all of my animal friends enjoying the farm they loved. At that moment, I was so deeply thinking inward and happy, I finally realized I had found my special purpose in life.

"I AM BERKLEY the GURU, and I am here to protect all my animal friends and show my human friends that there is a much, much better way!"

Finally, I found my cause, my purpose, and as I cuddled up for the night with my family, I could finally sleep with all the peace and love that is in my heart, because I finally know my purpose. I am not a failure, and our kind human friends will change, if we just show them the way!

THE END

AUTHORS NOTE:

For so many of us it is sometimes hard to find what we are good at or what our special talents are. Some go their whole lives and not find it but I have learned a lot from my dog Berkley. In this story Berkley shows us all that just being kind and motivated to act is one of the most special talents you can have in life.

This story was inspired by Berkley who yes, is a 100% real yellow Labrador career change dog who I was fortunate to adopt in 2013. The truth about Berkley is he loves all animals. He is calm, peaceful, loving and has naturally therapeutic quality to him that everyone immediately recognizes. The story is just a story but one I thought of because it's a type of story that I believe Berkley could make happen. I wanted to be able to share Berkley's love for animals and give him a voice to ask humans to be kind to all animals not just pets. Berkley has been a vegan for 2 years and has adjusted to his diet very well and this story hopes to inspire more people to see the benefits of veganism especially for reasons of animal welfare. Berkley's challenge to all of us is can we live together with the animals in kindness and peace in a vegan lifestyle so that no animals need to be harmed?

BTW, yes Berkley loves to FLOP!

BENEFITS OF VEGANISM

Veganism (a 100% plant-based diet) is more than just what we eat but encompasses a lifestyle that continually helps you make conscious, ethical, and informed decisions on how your choices impact animals, our environment, and our health. The 3 biggest benefits of going vegan is:

1) Animal Welfare: Berkley, like many others, believes that all animals deserve to be loved and not raised for food or consumer products.

2)Reducing the stress on the world's environment and natural resources. To raise animals for food and other products puts a tremendous strain on our environment and use of resources. By switching to a plant-based diet, you can make a positive impact on helping animals and the environment.

3)A plant-based vegan diet has numerous health benefits that can keep us healthy and living longer and more enriched lives.

If you are interested in learning more about Veganism, there are a lot of good resources out there, but I will mention one of mine and Berkley's favorite is: www.IloveVegan.com This site is a great resource to introduce you to the benefits of and how to transition to a vegan plant-based lifestyle.

Another one of of Berkley's favorites is an Instagram celebrity named Esther .the Wonder Pig. Please follow Esther and her friend Corno the Turkey. Berkley loves them!

Yes. Berkley also has an Instagram account. If you are interested in following him, please look up:
Berkley the Guru

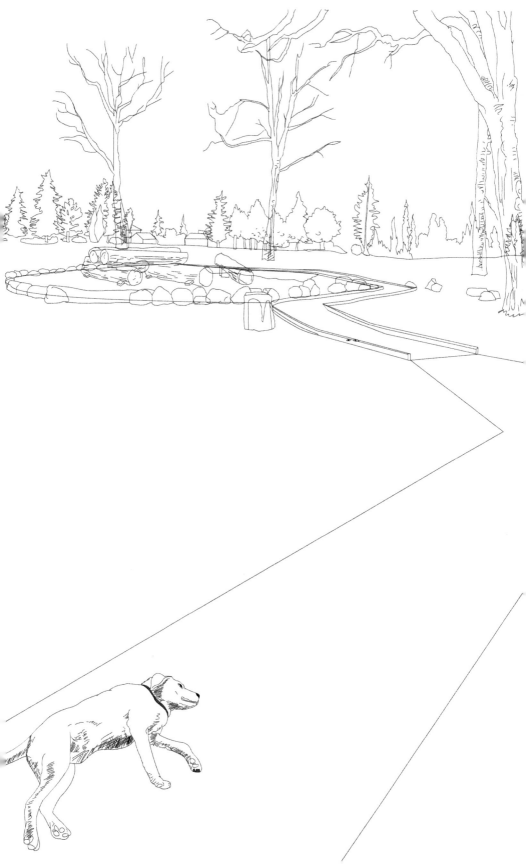

Visit
BerkleytheGuru.com
for updates on new adventures of
Berkley The Guru
coming soon!

Follow

BERKLEY THE GURU

On Instagram
&
Visit our Website

www.BerkleyTheGuru.com

CPSIA information can be obtained
at www.ICGtesting.com
Printed in the USA
LVHW051208020719
622877LV00015BC/152/P